Kylie Jean

Dancing Queen

by Marci Peschke

illustrated by Tuesday Mourning

PICTURE WINDOW BOOKS
a capstone imprint

Kylie Jean is published by Picture Window Books
A Capstone Imprint
1710 Roe Crest Drive
North Mankato, Minnesota 56003
www.capstonepub.com

Library of Congress Cataloging-in-Publication Data is available on the Library of
Congress website.

ISBN: 978-1-4048-6798-7 (library binding)
ISBN: 978-1-4048-7209-7 (paperback)

Summary: Kylie Jean wants to be a dancing queen as the star ballerina in Swan Lake.

Creative Director: Heather Kindseth
Graphic Designer: Emily Harris
Editor: Beth Brezenoff
Production Specialist: Danielle Ceminsky

Design Element Credit:
Shutterstock/blue67design

Printed in the United States of America in Stevens Point, Wisconsin
102011
006404WZS12

For Caitlyn
with love for Rick
—MP

Table of Contents

All About Me, Kylie Jean!

My name is Kylie Jean Carter. I live in a big, sunny, yellow house on Peachtree Lane in Jacksonville, Texas with Momma, Daddy, and my two brothers, T.J. and Ugly Brother.

T.J. is my older brother, and Ugly Brother is . . . well . . . he's really a dog. Don't you go telling him he is a dog. Okay? I mean it. He thinks he is a real true person.

He is a black-and-white bulldog. His front looks like his back, all smashed in. His face is all droopy like he's sad, but he's not.

His two front teeth stick out, and his tongue hangs down. (Now you know why his name is Ugly Brother.)

Everyone I love to the moon and back lives in Jacksonville. Nanny, Pa, Granny, Pappy, my aunts, my uncles, and my cousins all live here. I'm extra lucky, because I can see all of them any time I want to!

My momma says I'm pretty. She says I have eyes as blue as the summer sky and a smile as sweet as an angel. (Momma says pretty is as pretty does. That means being nice to the old folks, taking care of little animals, and respecting my momma and daddy.)

But I'm pretty on the outside and on the inside. My hair is long, brown, and curly.

I wear it in a ponytail sometimes, but my absolute most favorite is when Momma pulls it back in a princess style on special days.

I just gave you a little hint about my big dream. Ever since I was a bitty baby I have wanted to be an honest-to-goodness beauty queen. I even know the wave. It's side to side, nice and slow, with a dazzling smile. I practice all the time, because everybody knows beauty queens need to have a perfect wave.

I'm Kylie Jean, and I'm going to be a beauty queen. Just you wait and see!

Chapter One
Queen of the Crop

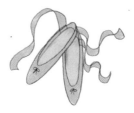

It's almost summertime, but this Saturday morning is cool and dewy.

My whole family — aunts, uncles, and a bunch of cousins — is at Lickskillet Farm. We're picking veggies from the huge garden patch.

Standing next to me is my best cousin, Lucy. Momma, Daddy, T.J. and Ugly Brother are here, too.

As far as I can see, row after row of green leafy tops fill the farm garden.

"Look at all these veggies," Pa crows. "This year we have a bumper crop! I'm going to have to give away carrots, peas, and greens," he adds, shaking his head. "There are just too many vegetables to can in jars or freeze for later."

I slip off my shoes and bury my feet in the soft, black dirt while Pa and Nanny decide which vegetables to pick.

Momma pulls on some red garden gloves with little green flowers. My gloves are pink, with little green flowers. Pink is my color, in case you didn't know.

Lucy fidgets and frowns. She points to the greens and says, "I sure hope we don't have to pick greens. I squish 'em every time!"

I nod. Greens are boring to pick.

Finally, Pa says, "T.J., you come with me to the cornfield. The rest of you, stay in the garden patch. My best girl can pick peas." He means my momma. He adds, "Kylie Jean and Lucy can pull carrots."

We shout, "Yippee!" Then we push a wheelbarrow down to the rows of carrots. Next to them, a scarecrow wearing one of Nanny's aprons, a hat, and some old cowboy boots dances in the breeze.

I get busy pulling carrots. That's more fun than pulling weeds! You can't eat weeds, but carrots are pretty tasty.

Suddenly, I see Ugly Brother. There's a big ole carrot hanging out of his mouth like a giant orange tongue. While we have been pulling the carrots, he has been eating them!

"Ugly Brother! Stop trying to eat all the carrots we just pulled," I shout, laughing. "They're still dirty, and you don't even like carrots!"

"Ruff," he barks. That means he doesn't want to stop eating carrots. But he moves away. Then he watches while we pick more carrots.

Some of the carrots are teeny-tiny babies, and some are giants as long as a grown-up's foot. I like the feathery green tops of the carrots best. They are so pretty, like lace on a Sunday dress.

I like picking carrots, but after a while, I get bored. Then T.J. comes over. He's here to boss me around. I just know it!

He says, "Hey, Lil' Bit, Pa told me to come help you." He frowns, looks at me, and adds, "No wonder you're so slow. You're wearin' a dress."

Putting my hands on my hips, I glare at T.J. "Hey, Lucy's wearin' a dress, too," I inform him. "We like dresses! They're not slowin' us down!"

"Let's have a picking contest," T.J. says. Then he starts pulling carrots to get a head start.

I shake my head. "No way," I tell him.

"You always win anyway!" Lucy mutters.

T.J. moves down the rows of carrots, pulling handfuls and tossing them on the ground. He is a fast carrot picker. Lucy is picking over on the next row, and she's been in the same spot ever since we got started. "You girls pick up the ones I pull out," T.J. tells us. "Then put them in the wheelbarrow."

Lucy and I look at each other. She shrugs. Neither of us wants to help T.J., but we don't have a choice.

"Okay," I say. "But we were doin' just fine before you got here."

As we pick up the carrots, Lucy asks, "Did you know that Madame Girard is planning a ballet performance of Swan Lake?"

Lucy is taking dance studio lessons from Madame Girard. Our friend Cara takes lessons there too. Momma says studio lessons are not in our budget, so I have been taking ballet classes at the Jacksonville Recreation Center for the last three months.

"Really? It sounds so pretty," I say, picturing a big white swan with a long smooth neck. "What's it about?" I ask.

Lucy says, "It's all about the beautiful Odette, Queen of the Swans, and her swan maidens. You won't believe it, but Odette and the maidens are enchanted, so by day they are swans, but at night they turn into beautiful girls. Real girls! Only a prince can break the evil spell."

I think I must be under a spell, too.

Just hearing the word queen puts me in a trance. Then an idea hits my brain like a bee on a blossom.

While Lucy watches, I make a green, lacy crown from the tops of some carrots. Then I do ballet turns down the carrot row.

T.J. rolls his eyes. He says, "Lil' Bit, how about more workin' and less dancing."

Lucy asks me, "Are you Odette?"

"Yup! I'm the swan queen," I tell her.

Suddenly, all I can think about is being Queen of the Swans.

Lucy smiles and shakes her head. She knows all about my big dream to be a beauty queen.

We see Pa's straw hat coming our way. Nanny thinks it's not fit for a scarecrow, but Pa loves that old hat.

He wants to check on us. Thanks to T.J., our wheelbarrow is so full that carrots are hanging over the sides. "Good work, kid!" he tells T.J. He gives Lucy a little squeezy hug. "I bet you helped a lot," he tells her. Lucy just grins.

Then he looks at me. I'm still wearing my carrot crown. I do a little twirl for him. Then Pa winks at me and says, "Sweet pea, you're the queen of the crop."

Chapter Two
Chicken Feather Tutus

After a big lunch of fried chicken, potato salad, and thick slices of juicy red tomatoes, Lucy and I go outside to play.

Lucy begs, "Let's to go to the chicken house to hunt for eggs."

I say, "I'm not too sure. Those chickens are mean. They don't like it when you take their eggs, and I don't blame them!"

The hen house is behind the barn. I take my time getting there by asking Lucy lots of questions about the swan queen.

I ask, "What part do you want in the ballet?"

"I think I'd like to be a beautiful swan maiden," Lucy answers.

We walk around the farmhouse. Nanny's flowers are growing so pretty. I love the pink daisies best. Lucy likes the roses.

"Let's pick Nanny a bouquet of flowers for her kitchen window!" I suggest.

Lucy nods. "That's a great idea!" she says.

Picking flowers in a sunny spot makes me happy. The flowers spread across the bed like a rainbow. Rows of orange tiger lilies, yellow tulips, purple iris, my pink daisies, and Lucy's old fashioned red roses curve around the back of the house.

The bees are buzzing all over the honeysuckle vine.

"Do you think drinking from the honeysuckle vine helps the bees make more honey?" Lucy asks, grabbing up some tall white flowers.

"I don't know," I admit. "I can't remember what we learned about honey bees."

I put my face close to the blooms and take a deep breath. The flowers smell like heaven.

"Ooooh, smell your flowers!" I tell Lucy. "They smell delightful!

When we have enough flowers to fill a fruit jar, we take them to the back door and lay them on the steps. Through the big kitchen window, I can hear Nanny and Momma talking while they wash the lunch dishes.

I stand under the window and shout, "Nanny, we picked you some flowers!"

"Thank you, darlin'!" Nanny shouts back.

"Come on," Lucy says. "Let's get those eggs."

Even before we get to the chicken house, I can hear the hens going cluck, cluck, cluck. There's a big fence around the chicken house. From the gate, I see the little wooden boxes that make up the chicken house. Each hen has her own box full of sweet yellow straw.

Some of the boxes are empty. Those hens are not at home. If they are not on their nests, it's easier to get the eggs. We have to be sneaky to get past the ones who are home.

Lucy grabs the egg basket from the gatepost. Then she pushes the gate open, pulling me behind her. "Here we go!" she whispers. "Cluck like a chicken. Maybe we can fool them."

"Cluck, cluck-cluck, bawk, bawk," I cackle.

The chickens look pretty nervous as we walk across the pen. Their beady black eyes follow us. Lucy walks faster, so she's already to the chicken house when a circle of chickens starts gathering around me.

"I'm pretty sure we aren't fooling them," I say. "I'm trapped!"

The hens start to crowd around the chicken house steps, too. They want to see what Lucy is doing. I think they know that she's loading up her basket with their eggs. That's when I see a whole lot of white chicken feathers on the ground. An idea hits my brain like eggs on an iron skillet.

"Lucy, come quick! I got a plan," I shout. That makes the chickens run away.

Lucy turns around, smiling. She holds up her basket. It's full of eggs. "I've got twelve eggs in this basket. That's a bunch," she brags.

"Come on!" I say. I am picking up chicken feathers as fast as I can.

Lucy looks puzzled. "We came for eggs, not feathers," she says.

"I know, but these feathers will make two fine feather tutus just perfect for swan queens," I explain quickly, keeping my eyes on the chickens.

Lucy's eyes get big. She knows what I want to do! We gather up a whole pile of the feathers.

"I wish we had real tutus to glue them on," I say sadly.

"We could tuck them up under the sashes of our dresses," Lucy suggests.

I gasp. "That's the best idea you've had all day, Lucy!" I say. "Why didn't I think of that?"

Twirling, twirling, twirling, we dance around in our chicken feather tutus. We twirl till we fall over in a heap, giggling.

A shadow falls over us. It's T.J.

"Momma wants you," he says. Then he frowns. "What are you doing? Are you pretending to be that big bird that stands in front of the Chicken Bucket?" he asks, laughing.

"Can't you tell?" I say. T.J. can be so annoying. "We're beautiful swans!"

T.J. snorts. "Chickens are not the same as swans," he says. "Anyway, it's time to go. And Lil' Bit, if Momma sees those dirty feathers on your good dress, you're gonna be in big trouble!"

Chapter Three

The First Rule

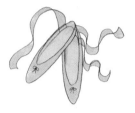

On Monday night, Lucy calls me on the phone. "Guess what?" she says.

I think for a second. "Did you get a new cat?" I ask.

"Nope," Lucy says. "Better."

"Did you find ten dollars?" I ask.

"Nope," Lucy says. "Better!"

"Did your momma win the lottery?" I ask.

Lucy laughs. "No, silly," she says. "Give up?"

"I give up!" I tell her.

"Tonight, after our dance lesson, Madame told us she needs so many dancers for the ballet that she is holding open auditions," Lucy tells me. I can hear from her voice that she's smiling.

My mouth drops open. "Are you joking?" I ask. "Is it true? Is Madame having open auditions? Can I try out to be in the ballet?"

"I knew you'd be excited!" she says. "Yes, it's true!"

After I hang up, I am so excited I can't believe it. "Ugly Brother! Ugly Brother!" I shout.

He pads sleepily past me and plops down on the floor next to my pink backpack.

I sit down beside him. "Guess what?" I say. "I'm going to audition for Swan Lake. Can't you just see me as the swan queen?"

He does not seem excited. In fact, he turns around, ignoring me.

"I don't like talking to your tail," I tell him. "What's wrong with you, Ugly Brother? Aren't you happy for me?"

Ugly Brother just whines. He must be sad about something. "Maybe a doggie treat will cheer you up," I say.

I get one from the kitchen, but he doesn't even lick it, so he must not be hungry.

It's cool in the house, so he's not too hot. Just from looking at him I can see that he probably just had a nap, so he can't be sleepy.

Finally, it hits me like rain in June.

"I know!" I shout. "You want to be a ballerina, too, just like me! Right, Ugly Brother? Is that what's wrong?"

Ugly Brother stands up and wags his tail. "Ruff ruff!" he barks. One bark means no. Two barks means yes!

"Okay," I tell him. "Don't worry. I'll teach you all the rules you need to know."

Ugly Brother barks twice. He's excited to learn all about being a ballerina. And I'm pretty excited to teach him!

Then I say, "Rule number one is a very important rule. Look at my feet." Then I point my toes. "Rule number one: Ballerinas always point their toes."

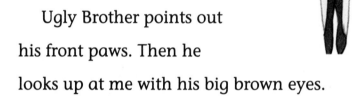

Ugly Brother points out his front paws. Then he looks up at me with his big brown eyes.

I pat him on the head. "Good job!" I say. "Now you're on your way to being a real true ballerina." And, I think to myself, I am one pirouette away from being the swan queen.

Chapter Four
Ballet Lessons

After school on Tuesday, Momma drives me
over to the rec center for my dance lesson. When
we get to the rec center there are girls everywhere;
short, tall, round, and
skinny as a stick. Some
girls are wearing T-shirts
and shorts, and some are
wearing leotards with tutus.
I have on my black shorts
and a pink princess shirt
with a sparkly silver crown.

I walk over and sit down on one of the wooden benches that line the room. Then I look around the dance studio.

It is really just a big bright room. Before it was the dance studio, it was a senior center, so they had to hang mirrors on one wall and put a long barre down the center of the room.

Little ballerinas are holding the barre as they plié, bending down low with their toes and knees pointed out. Some of the other girls are holding the barre as they practice standing on their toes. The older girls pirouette around the studio in their toe shoes.

Some of the older ballerinas have practiced a lot! They float through the air, light as a feather. Then they glide into their next move.

I watch them while I get my ballet shoes out of my bag. They are my cousin Lilly's old ballet slippers.

After I slide my feet into the slippers, I slowly and very carefully wind the long pink ribbons around my ankles, then tie the bows. I slip my bag under the bench, and then I am ready to go to the barre to take my place next to my friend Katie.

I make sure my feet are in the correct position as I bend low. In my head, I'm thinking *plié one, plié two, plié three*.

"Do you know about the auditions for Swan Lake?" Katie whispers.

"I sure do!" I whisper back. "Odette is the perfect part for me, since I'm going to be a queen."

Katie smiles. "I thought your cousin Lilly would get the part for Odette. I didn't know you'd try out too!" she says. When I nod, she says, "Good luck!"

"Shhh!" says our teacher, Ms. Dixie.

Ms. Dixie is tall like a tree. She is wearing a pink leotard and a long pink skirt and white toe shoes. The shoes are worn and scuffed.

As she moves around the room, she quietly talks to each girl. "You're a natural ballerina, Kylie Jean! Just look at your graceful arms," she tells me.

"Thank you," I say. "I always knew I was going to be a ballerina — and a beauty queen, of course."

Ms. Dixie just smiles and walks to the next girl.

When we're done warming up, Ms. Dixie calls, "Ballerinas gather around. I have an exciting announcement. Madame Girard wants you all to try out for a part in her recital of Swan Lake! The auditions are Saturday at nine a.m."

I know what part I want already! Odette is the lead role, so I will need to practice a lot of ballet moves. I decide I better ask for help. I raise my hand and ask, "Can you help me be Odette?"

Ms. Dixie claps her hands. "What a wonderful idea, Kylie Jean!" she exclaims. "We can all practice the dance steps. That way, everyone will be ready to try out!"

The other ballerinas all clap and cheer.

That's not what I meant at all! But I guess I don't care, as long as I get time to practice.

Chapter Five
School Surprise

The next morning, as soon as we get to our classroom, Cara, Lucy, and I start talking about the ballet. But when class starts, I can't stop thinking about being the Swan Queen.

Today Ms. Corazón tells our class she has a surprise for us. We beg her to tell us what it is, but she just smiles and says, "You will just have to wait until the end of the day."

At lunchtime, in the big, noisy cafeteria, Lucy, Paula, Cara, and I sit together. We try to guess what the surprise is.

"Maybe it's going to be free day on Friday," Cara says.

"Maybe we're going to get to go read to the kindergarten class," I say.

"Maybe we're getting a free homework pass," Lucy says.

"Maybe we're having a party!" Cara says.

Paula shakes her head. "I think you're all wrong. We'll just have to wait for our teacher to tell us," she says.

All afternoon, everyone's trying to figure out what the surprise is.

Finally, at the end of the day, Ms. Corazón passes out permission slips. She announces, "On Friday, the second grade is taking a field trip to see the ballet! We'll be seeing Cinderella. Isn't this exciting news, class?"

Before I can stop myself, I squeal! Queens are not squealers. Quickly, I cover my mouth with my hand.

I don't think anyone noticed. The girls are all too busy being excited. The boys don't seem too thrilled, though.

As for me, I can't wait. Watching the ballerinas might help me when I try out for the part of Odette. I can't believe how lucky I am!

"This is a dream come true! I can't wait to see the dancers," I say.

Lucy just keeps repeating, "I can hardly believe it. Pinch me!"

Paula finally does pinch her, but not too hard. She's just teasing.

Cara tells us, "One time my grandma took me to the ballet in the big city. The costumes the ballerinas wear are amazing! They have every color, with silk flowers sewn into their tutus. I think I'd want a blue one."

Lucy says, "I would love a purple tutu."

I bet you already know what color tutu I want.

That's right.

Pink!

When I get home, Momma is in the kitchen, rolling out biscuit dough.

I ask, "Momma, do you think you could sign my permission slip? It's to go to the ballet."

Momma signs her name in big, curly letters. When she hands the slip back to me, I put it right into my backpack. I don't want it to get lost!

Chapter Six
Seeing Cinderella

When we get off the bus in front of the ballet on Friday morning, I'm so excited that I feel like I could float away like a feather. Going to the ballet is a dream come true! Putting my hands over my head, I do a twirl on the sidewalk.

Lucy, Katie, and Cara are right next to me. On field trips we have the buddy system. I want to have Lucy for a buddy, but Cara gets Lucy and I get Katie.

The Performance Center is gigantic. It even has rows of seats upstairs. I hope we get to sit there!

A nice lady in a red jacket hands us each a program. That's a little book about the ballet.

Ms. Corazón tells us that we can use the program to follow the ballet and learn about the dancers.

I am disappointed when the lady in the red jacket leads us to our seats downstairs in the second row. At least we are close to the front.

Suddenly, we hear music coming from a big hole in front of the stage. Musicians sit there to play music for the ballerinas without distracting the folks watching them dance. I know I would rather watch the dancers!

The lights go down. Right away, it feels colder in the big room. Momma made me bring a sweater, so I put it on.

Then the curtains open, and I forget everything else.

Cara was right about the costumes. The stepsisters and the mean old stepmother are wearing the most beautiful costumes I've ever seen. But poor Cinderella! Her costume is an ugly brown dress without a tutu. Can you believe it?

The ballerinas float across the stage, telling the story of Cinderella through their dancing.

Cinderella dances with a broom, cleaning the house for her stepmother. I know that later she will get to dance with the prince. I watch carefully as the story goes on.

Then they suddenly stop dancing and the lights go up.

"What happened?" I ask. "What's going on? We didn't even get to see the prince yet!"

Ms. Corazón says, "Don't worry! The prince will come in the second act. This is a break they call intermission. You can use this time to read the program."

"Hey, guess what? It says in the program the part of Cinderella is performed by a prima ballerina!" Cara tells me. "Her name is Lizette Blanc."

"Oh, I sure hope we can meet her!" I say.

Soon, the lights turn off again. I look at Cinderella on the stage.

Her godmother helped her get ready for the ball. She looks real pretty with her dark hair up in a bun. Her white gown is long and she is wearing a sparkly tiara. Oooh, I just love tiaras! I hope Odette wears one.

The music starts. Right away, I'm lost in the fairy tale story. The ballroom scene is filled with so many costumes that I can't even see them all! Finally, the prince finds Cinderella.

The glass slipper fits her. Then they live happily ever after.

The ballet is over. The curtains go down and then they go right back up again. All of the dancers are on stage. They hold hands and bow.

My friends and I stand up and clap and clap. Even Cole and the other boys clap. Maybe they like ballet after all.

Then Ms. Corazón announces, "We are in for a treat! The prima ballerina, Lizette Blanc, is waiting to say hello to us." We all hurry, trying to move ahead, anxious to see her.

When we see her, Lizette Blanc looks as lovely as she did on stage, but now she is surrounded by school kids instead of princesses.

Soon it's my turn to talk to Lizette. I say, "Ever since I was an itty bitty baby I've wanted to be a queen, just like Cinderella. You found your prince and made your dream come true."

She smiles and asks, "Are you looking for a prince?"

"No, not really," I say. "But if I have to dance with one to wear a tiara, I will!" Then I tell her all about my plans to be Odette.

"Hurry up, Kylie Jean!" Lucy says. She is tapping me on the shoulder. I know she wants her turn, but Lizette is so nice! I hate to go.

Lucy steps up next to me.

"Miss Lizette, my turn is over, but this is my best cousin, Lucy," I say.

"You will be a wonderful Odette, little ballerina. Remember to point your toes!" Miss Lizette says.

"I will," I tell her. "I promise!"

Chapter Seven
Bubble Buns

That night at supper I tell Momma, Daddy, T.J., and Ugly Brother all about the ballet.

"The Jacksonville Performance Center is better than the movie theater," I say.

Momma nods. "Your daddy and I saw a play there," she says. "It's very nice."

"I was shocked when Cinderella didn't have a tutu on her first costume," I go on. "But later she had on a long white gown and a sparkly tiara. It had so many tiny little diamonds. They looked like stars!"

Daddy says, "Sounds like you had a wonderful time, sugar."

"Yup, I sure did," I reply. Then I remember something else. "Miss Lizette Blanc, the prima ballerina, wears her hair in a bun. Momma, can you put my hair in a bun?"

Momma nods. Everyone at the table is finished, but I've been talking so much that I still have a lot of food on my plate.

"Maybe you should eat some supper now," Daddy suggests. "You can save some of this story for later."

Under the table, Ugly Brother barks twice. I guess he wants me to stop talking and eat, too.

"Okay, Daddy," I say. I start eating my veggies.

Between bites, I remind everyone that auditions for Swan Lake are tomorrow at nine o'clock. "Maybe I should go to bed right after I eat," I say, scooping up some peas.

"That's a little too early for bedtime. Why don't you help me with the dishes first?" Daddy says.

Daddy and I do the dishes. First I clear the table. Then I help him put the dishes into the dishwasher after he rinses them off. I like to put the spoons, forks, and knives in the little silverware baskets. I put all the spoons together so they can keep each other company. Then I do the same for the knives and forks, too.

When we're all done with the dishes, we watch TV. I only watch one show. Then Momma asks me, "Are you ready to take a bath now?"

"I sure am!" I say. I get up and head for the stairs.

Ugly Brother follows me. He likes to go with me when I take a bath. T.J. says Ugly Brother wants to drink the bathwater that spills on the floor, but I know it's because Ugly Brother really likes to bring me a towel. Sometimes he does lap up the bathwater a little bit, too.

"A bubble bath would be nice," I say. "What do you think, Ugly Brother?"

"Ruff, ruff," he barks. Two barks means yes!

I start to run the water. When it's nice and steamy, I pour in the bubble bath. But I put a little extra in by accident. It will be okay, since we like a lot of bubbles.

I get in the tub. Then I get a great idea. "Ugly Brother, I am going to give you the next rule for being a ballerina," I declare. "It is rule number two."

He gets real excited and jumps up on the edge of the tub. "Ruff, ruff!" he barks happily.

"Here it is, rule number two. Ballerinas have hair buns," I tell him. "I am going to have to get a hair bun tomorrow for my audition."

Then I pull my hair up in a pile on top of my head. "See? This is a bun," I say.

He whines and tries to stick his head under my pink towel. Oh no! This one will be hard for him, because he doesn't have much hair. Then an idea hits me like suds in a carwash.

"Come here," I say. Ugly Brother sits down right next to the tub. I pick up a big handful of bubbles and swirl them on top of his head.

"There you go, Ugly Brother!" I say. "You have your very own hair bun!"

He is so happy he chases his tail in a circle. Then he drags my pink towel over and holds it up to me. Bath time is over.

Later, with my head on my soft feather pillow, I drift off to sleep, thinking about being Queen of the Swans.

Chapter Eight
Dance Auditions

The next morning, I walk everywhere on my tiptoes. At the breakfast bar in the kitchen, I do a plié.

Momma says, "Honey, go wake up T.J. He has a game today and your daddy is waiting for him."

I tell her, "Okay, but I'm going to practice on my way, 'cause I have to be ready for tryouts."

I pirouette right before going up the stairs. I turn and do a plié on each step. On the first step, I say, "Plié one." On the next step, I say, "Plié two." On the third step, I say, "Plié three."

Momma yells, "Hurry up, Kylie Jean!"

I don't do any more pliés. I just run up the steps.

After I knock on T.J.'s door, I do a perfect arabesque, stretching my arm out and my leg behind me with carefully pointed toes.

"T.J.!" I yell. "Momma says you're gonna be late for the soccer tournament, so wake up!"

Two seconds later, he almost knocks me over as he runs out of his room. "What time is it?" he asks.

From downstairs, Daddy shouts, "Hurry up, son! It's eight o'clock! I'll be waiting in the car."

My tummy is rumbling, so I go downstairs and start eating breakfast while T.J. gets ready.

When he runs down the stairs, I say, "Good luck! I hope your team wins." He smiles, gives me a high five, and dashes out the door. Then it's just Momma and me.

I'm getting so nervous! It feels like I have a stomach full of June bugs.

Momma brushes my shiny brown hair and puts it up in a bun. Then I get dressed. I'm wearing my black shorts and my pink t-shirt with the princess crown on the front for good luck. I have my ballet slippers tucked into my bag.

Finally, it's time to go!

Madame Girard's dance studio is in an old house. The bottom floor is where the dance lessons are. Madame lives upstairs. In the studio, the walls are all painted a pink as soft as rose petals.

The room is full of dancers. All of Madame's girls are wearing black leotards and pink tutus. I can tell that most of the girls who take classes with Ms. Dixie, like I do, are wearing shorts.

The older girls are warming up at the barre. I see my cousin Lilly there. She looks beautiful! Littler girls are doing pliés and stretching. I look around the room for Lucy. I'm as nervous as a cat in a bathtub.

"You'll be awesome," Momma tells me. "Just dance your best." Then she gives me a little push forward, and I go to stretch with the younger girls.

Madame watches with a clipboard from the corner of the room. She is tiny and dressed all in black. Her black hair is in a ballerina bun and her black eyes don't miss anything.

Once we are all done stretching, Madame says, "You will each announce the part you are trying out for. Then you will dance."

The older girls dance first. My cousin Lilly takes my breath away! She flits across the room like she has butterfly wings. When she dances it is just like seeing Lizette Blanc.

When it is time for the younger girls we all warm up at the barre together.

Then Madame calls my name.

As I take the floor, I softly say, "I am dancing the part of Odette."

Madame frowns a little when she hears me. Lilly winks at me.

Counting my steps quietly under my breath, I begin.

Then suddenly there is nothing but the dance. It seems like I just started when I end with a jump followed by an arabesque.

No one claps or cheers. I know that Madame would not allow it. It's so quiet you could hear the feathers on hummingbird wings.

Momma is smiling at me. Madame smiles too, just a little, and marks something on her clipboard.

After everyone dances, Madame announces, "I will post the parts for the ballet on Monday."

I whisper, "That seems like one hundred days from now. How can I wait until Monday?"

Katie groans. "I don't know," she says. "It's a long, long time to wait."

I grab my bag and follow Momma out to the van. We head home.

Momma says, "Time will pass faster than you think."

I sure hope she's right.

Chapter Nine
Not Odette

On Monday right after school, I ride my bike all the way over to Madame's dance studio. I speed down Peachtree Street with my pink handlebar streamers blowing in the wind. Ugly Brother has to run to follow me. He can hardly keep up.

When we get to Madame's studio, I hop off my bike and sprint to the door. A creamy piece of paper is tacked to it.

In curly black writing are the names of all of the ballerinas, and next to them are the parts in the ballet.

I look for my name, but the first name on the list is Lilly. She will be playing Odette.

My heart sinks way down to my toes.

It says "swan maiden" next to my name. Katie, Lucy, and Cara are all swan maidens too.

"Ugly Brother, I'm not the swan queen," I say sadly. "I'm just a swan maiden. I can't believe it. I didn't get to be Odette."

Ugly Brother just whines and puts his paws over his face. Crying a little, I sit down on the porch steps. Ugly Brother comes over to lick my face. He can tell I'm as sad as a dog who's lost his bone.

"We can't cry all day, Ugly Brother," I say, wiping my face with my shirt. "I'm happy for Lilly. She should be Odette."

Then I think of something. "Maybe this is a good time to tell you the next rule for being a ballerina!"

"Ruff, ruff!" says Ugly Brother.

"Rule number three is: Ballerinas are always graceful. It's okay to get a smaller part if a better ballerina gets the big one," I explain. "You just have to be graceful. When I get home, I'll call Lilly and tell her congratulations. She earned the part of the queen. Now I'll show you how to dance gracefully," I add. "Just watch me!"

He barks, "Ruff, ruff."

I do a perfect arabesque. Ugly Brother tries to do a turn, but he just looks like he's chasing his tail! He is not a graceful dancer, but at least he knows the main rules for being a ballerina.

Besides, he acts graceful lots of times by being nice. I pat him on the head and say, "Good job, Ugly Brother!"

Seems to me you can be a chicken one day and feathers the next or a dog one day and a ballerina the next.

Chapter Ten
Practice Makes Perfect

For the next two weeks, I will have ballet practice two times a week! I have to go to classes with Ms. Dixie and with Madame.

Ballet practice with Madame is on Thursday and Friday. When I arrive at the dance studio, the only people there are the other girls performing in Swan Lake. My cousins Lilly and Lucy smile at me and Lilly gives a little wave.

Madame begins to give us drills to do. These are just dance steps that we repeat a bunch of times. She counts in French. "Un, deux, trois."

She has a long black stick, and she taps it on the floor as she counts. The tapping of the stick makes it hard to concentrate, and my feet get all tangled up. I made a mistake. My feet are in the wrong position.

Madame sees them with her dark bird-like eyes. Madame sees everything all the time.

The tapping stick stops. Madame asks the ballerinas to sit. She adds coldly, "Everyone except Kylie Jean, *s'il vous plait.*" When I frown, she says, "That means 'please.'" Then she makes me repeat the dance step over and over.

Madame says, " Again, again, again!" She points to my legs and feet with the black stick. My feet find the right position. Carefully, I repeat it again and again.

I am so embarrassed, even when Madame finally says, "*Tres bien.*" That means very good, but I just feel bad.

When I finally get to join the younger girls on the bench, I whisper, "I wish I was back in Ms. Dixie's class!"

Katie says, "I know. Me too!"

I think to myself that it can't be worth it to keep coming for lessons if Madame gets so mad when I make a little mistake.

Then I remember something. I'm doing all of this to be a swan maiden. I wished I could be in Swan Lake.

Getting my wish means I have to try to be the best swan maiden ever.

For the rest of our lesson, I listen to everything Madame says. My eyes are on her and on Lilly at all times. You can learn a lot just by watching.

By the end of our lesson, I can tell I'm getting better! My feet know the steps, even when I feel nervous.

Lucy whispers, "You're looking like a real true swan maiden, Kylie Jean."

Momma walks into the studio to pick me up. I run through the dance steps one more time.

Watching me dance, Momma's face lights up like a firefly.

When Madame nods her head, signaling that I can go, I grab my ballet bag.

Outside on the porch, Momma gives me a big old squeezy hug. She whispers, "You are a beautiful little ballerina. I am so proud of you!"

"Thanks, Momma," I say, smiling. "At first, it was really hard, and I made a mistake."

"But you kept trying, right?" Momma asks. I nod, and she says, "That's the part that proves you're a real ballerina."

Chapter Eleven
A Prince for Odette

When we get to Madame's studio on Friday, there are ballerinas waiting on her porch. It seems like everyone is outside.

"Where is Madame?" I ask Momma.

Momma shrugs. "She didn't call to cancel your lesson," she says, "so I guess she's just running late."

We weave our way up the steps through groups of tutus. Lilly and Lucy make their way toward us.

"Hey, Kylie Jean. Hi, Aunt Shelly," Lucy says.

Lilly smiles and takes my hand. "Don't worry," she tells Momma. "I'll look after Kylie Jean."

Momma says, "Aren't you sweet, Lilly! Thank you for keeping an eye on her. I'm going to run over to the Piggly Wiggly. I'll be back after class." Momma leaves. Then Lilly and Lucy and I sit down and chat for a while.

When Madame arrives a few minutes later, she seems strange. Her hair is messy and she isn't wearing her ballet slippers like she always does.

We start practicing, and she holds the clipboard, but she doesn't notice any mistakes because she is staring into space. Several times, she loses count with the black stick. Her tapping sounds more like rain than rhythm.

What's wrong with Madame? She doesn't even notice the hum of the ballerinas whispering. I wonder if Madame is sick.

Finally, I can't stand it anymore. I have to know what's going on, so I go to right up to her. Madame doesn't see me at first, but Lilly does. Lilly waves at me to come back to the barre. Shaking my head, I wait. It takes a while, but finally, Madame sees me.

"Yes, Kylie Jean, what is it?" she asks.

"Are you okay, Madame?" I ask quietly.

I am shocked when Madame crumples. She sits down on the bench. She doesn't cry, but she looks like she wants to. She even covers her face with her hands. The dancers have stopped dancing. They start walking over.

"My beautiful dancers, there is a big problem!" Madame confesses. "The boy who was going to be the prince has broken his ankle. He may never dance again. It is so sad."

I gasp. Everyone begins to whisper. One little ballerina starts to cry.

We have worked so hard! I kind of want to cry too, but beauty queens are never quitters.

"Our ballet is ruined!" Madame says. "We can't perform Swan Lake without a prince for Odette."

One girl asks, "Can another girl dance the role of the prince?"

Madame shakes her head and explains, "The prince must lift Odette many, many times. None of you are strong enough to be the prince."

We all think some more, but no one has any good ideas. Finally, Madame claps her hands. "We are done for today," she says. "Class is dismissed. I have to think!"

Momma is not here to pick me up yet, so Lilly, Lucy, and I sit on the porch waiting for her. We are all too sad to talk much. This is Lilly's big chance to be the prima ballerina, and my first chance to be a swan maiden. I don't want it to be ruined.

Lilly tries to cheer us up. She says, "Madame will figure it out. Don't worry."

"I wish that boy didn't break his ankle," Lucy says.

I nod and say, "Me too, but we can't change it, so we have to find a new prince. Right?"

When Momma pulls up, I wave goodbye to my cousins. "Don't worry, Lilly," I say. "I'm gonna think of a plan so you get to be Odette."

All the way home, I think about boys I know. I have lots of friends who are boys, but none of them seem like ballerinas.

At home, after I help Momma bring in the groceries, I get a purple Popsicle from one of the bags. Ugly Brother and I have the Popsicle on the back steps. I have a lick and then he has one. I like sharing Popsicles with Ugly Brother.

I tell Ugly Brother all about our ballet boy troubles. He whines a little, but I'm not sure if he feels bad for us or if he just wants more of the Popsicle.

"You want another lick?" I ask, holding out the frozen treat.

He barks excitedly, "Ruff, ruff." Then he bites the end off.

"Popsicles are for licking!" I say.

But I can't be mad at Ugly Brother. He just likes purple Popsicles, and so do I.

Then T.J. walks up. When he sees all the purple sweetness on my face and on Ugly Brother's, he laughs. "You've got doggie germs now," he teases me. "You're probably gonna grow a tail."

When I look up at T.J., an idea hits my brain like syrup on a snow cone. I whisper to Ugly Brother, "Are you thinking what I'm thinking?"

"Ruff, ruff!" he barks.

You just know I have a plan to get a prince for Odette! I tell T.J. all about our ballerina problem and how sad Lilly is. Lilly is one of his favorite cousins. He seems real sorry, but doesn't offer to help.

I take a deep breath. This isn't easy. Then I say, "You could be the prince. None of your friends would ever see you dancin', because they don't go to the ballet anyway. It would make all the ballerinas so happy, especially Lilly."

"I'm not a dancer," he says.

"You wouldn't have to do much dancing," I say.

He frowns, but I can tell he's thinking about it. "What would I have to do?" he asks.

"You would be lifting Lilly while she dances," I explain. "And since you're real strong I know you can do it for sure."

T.J. hesitates. "I don't know," he says. "I'm not a dancer." He thinks for a long, long time. At first I think he's going to say no. Then he takes a deep breath and says, "Let's make a deal. Will you promise to clean my room for a whole month?"

I snort. "Some deal!" I mutter. "I'd rather clean out Granny's cat box for a month!"

But what can I do? We have to have a prince.

So I stick out my hand and say, "We better shake on it."

Chapter Twelve

A Princess After All

T.J. comes with me to Madame Girard's studio next time we have practice. He looks funny, standing there in his gray sweat pants with ballerinas all around him. He's usually on the soccer field surrounded by big, sweaty soccer players. Lilly looks shocked to see him!

I take T.J.'s hand and pull him over to Madame.

"Who is this?" she asks, frowning.

"This is the new prince!" I tell her. "My very own brother, T.J. Carter, is going to be a ballerina. But we can't tell anyone! Okay?"

T.J. turns as red as a robin's belly and shuffles his feet.

Madame gushes, "I am so thrilled!"

"I still have to make time for soccer practice," T.J. says. "I'm just doing this dancing thing to help out my sister and my cousin Lilly."

"I promise to work around your soccer schedule for your lessons," Madame says.

T.J. and Lilly already know each other, so they'll be good partners. Lilly squeals and gives T.J. a big hug when she finds out he'll be the prince.

Madame tells me, "Your brother is perfect. He is an athlete, so he will have no trouble lifting Lilly."

During practice, Madame spends all of her time working with T.J. and Lilly.

T.J. is a quick learner, and luckily he doesn't have to do much. Mostly, he is just there for the lifts.

Lucy, Cara, Katie, and I are practicing too. Our big part is dancing around Odette when she is changing from a swan to a girl. We have to make a little half circle around her.

Since Lilly is busy practicing with T.J., we pretend that a stool is Odette. We all move forward together, reaching out our arms like fluttering wings.

Gathering around the stool, we wait for Odette and the prince to dance together.

Finally, when they do, we swan maidens leap joyfully in the background.

When we are done with the rehearsal, Madame claps her hands. Her eyes sparkle, and she says, "Kylie Jean, getting your brother to be the prince is a real feather in your cap! You saved our ballet!"

Everyone begins to take off their ballet slippers and pack up their bags. Lucy and I sit side by side, best ballerina buddies and best cousins.

T.J. is talking to Lilly about their dance. They are best cousins too. It is nice to have such a big family. When someone needs help, all we have to do is ask and usually someone figures out how to help, just like T.J. and me.

Madame calls out, "We only have one practice session left, tomorrow afternoon. On Saturday morning at nine o'clock, we'll have a dress rehearsal at the high school. I will see you then, dancers. *Au revoir.* Goodbye!"

I can't wait to see my costume. It will be all white because I'm a swan maiden. And I bet it'll be a lot better than chicken feathers. I lean over to Lucy and whisper, "No more farm tutus for us!"

I am very excited. If T.J. is a prince, then that makes me a princess!

Chapter Thirteen
Dress Rehearsal

Early next Saturday morning, Momma makes pancakes that are light as a feather. She mixes them in a big blue bowl and I get to pour the milk in. Then we make giant pancakes as big as a plate on our old black griddle.

I'm standing on my stepstool, reaching for the syrup, when T.J. walks into the kitchen.

He laughs. Then he reaches over my head, saying, "I've got this one, shorty!"

T.J. puts the maple syrup on the table. Then he pulls out a chair and sits down. Daddy walks in, too.

"I helped make the pancakes," I announce.

"They look delicious!" Daddy says.

He puts the plate of pancakes on the table. Then Momma brings a plate piled high with crispy bacon. We all start eating.

Pretty soon, we hear Ugly Brother begging for some bacon. Momma gives me a stern look because she knows I want to feed him under the table.

Daddy asks, "T.J., what will your friends on the football team have to say about you being in the ballet?"

"I don't know," T.J. says. "But it's a lot harder than it looks. I've only been to a couple of lessons, and I have to be ready for the performance. I don't want to let Madame, Lilly, and Kylie Jean down."

Momma checks her watch. Then she says, "You two better hurry and eat your breakfast or you'll be late for rehearsal!"

Soon, the empty plates are stacked in the kitchen sink. T.J. will drive us to the high school.

When we get there, he lets me out in front of the doors and then goes to park his truck.

We will rehearse and perform in the high school auditorium. It's nice, but not as nice as the Jacksonville Performance Center where we went to see Cinderella.

As I'm going up to the front door, I turn to look for T.J., but he's nowhere to be seen! I don't even spot his truck in the parking lot. I see girls rushing all over the place, but I don't see my brother.

Lucy runs up to me, holding out her extra tutu and leotard. I am borrowing them for the ballet. "I can't find my brother," I tell Lucy.

She doesn't look worried. "He probably went to park somewhere else," she says. "So his friends won't know he's here if they happen to drive by."

I smack my forehead. "Of course!" I say. "Oh, Lucy, you have set my mind at ease." Then Lucy and I head inside the school.

All of the swan maidens are wearing beautiful headbands with white feathers and leotards and fluffy tutus.

You won't believe it, but makeup is part of our costume too! I never get to wear makeup. The older ballerinas help us put it on in the dressing room. The dressing room is really one of the locker rooms, but we can pretend we are backstage at a big, fancy theater.

Lilly puts white powder all over my face. The she adds some pink to my cheeks and lips. She tells me, "Keep your hands off of your face, or you'll mess up my excellent makeup job. Okay? And be careful to not get any water on your face, either."

I gasp when I see my face in the mirror. "I look so pretty!" I whisper. "I want to look like this forever. I'll never take a bath again!"

Lilly laughs. "You can always put on more makeup later, and baths are important," she tells me. "Especially bubble baths."

I have to remember to share this new rule with Ugly Brother! Rule number four: Ballerinas get to wear beautiful makeup. Ugly Brother can wear lipstick if he doesn't try to eat it first.

I leave the locker room and see T.J. walking down the hall.

He's wearing tights, pants that go to his knees, a white ruffled shirt, and a sky-blue vest. His face is white as a clean cotton sheet.

Lilly comes out and stands next to him. She looks so beautiful that when I see her I forget she's my cousin. She looks like a real, true queen!

We all go into the auditorium. Tapping her black stick on the stage, Madame calls out, "Places, everyone! We are ready to begin our ballet."

I do not make one mistake during the whole entire dress rehearsal. Not even a little tiny one. T.J. has to repeat his entrance twice, but his lifts are awesome.

After we're all done, Madame tells us that we are ready for our big day. Clapping her hands, she exclaims, "The performance will be wonderful, *magnifique!*"

Chapter Fourteen
Swan Lake

That night, right before the performance, Lilly looks calm and beautiful. She really is a prima ballerina. But Madame Girard is as nervous as a cat in a car.

She keeps checking on things. First she checks on the music. Then she checks with the set crew. After that she talks to all the ballerinas and T.J., too.

Everyone gets a final check from Madame Girard. She checks to make sure our makeup is perfect and that our tutus have no rips.

She looks at me first. Then, while she checks Cara, Lucy, and Katie, I peek through the curtain.

There are a ton of people here! I see Momma, Daddy, Nanny, Pa, Granny, and Pappy. Plus all of my aunts and uncles and cousins and friends.

It is so exciting to dance for all the people I love to the moon and back! I wish Ugly Brother could see me dance too, but dogs are not allowed at the ballet.

All of us swan maidens sit down on a bench backstage, waiting. We smile and swing our legs, swaying together in our fluffy tutus.

I thought I would be nervous, but I'm having too much fun to get butterflies in my tummy. Sometimes it is better to not be the queen! Can you believe I said that?

Then Ms. Dixie comes back to check on all of her ballerinas. "Y'all are going to be amazing swan maidens!" she exclaims.

Then she gives each of us a big squeezy hug. When she hugs me, she whispers, "You make me proud out there, you hear?"

Just then Madame Girard says, "*Vite, vite!*" That means hurry up fast in French.

It is time for the ballet to begin.

As we line up to go onto the stage, Madame reminds us, "Ballerinas, be sure to point your toes! And reach your arms all the way to the tips of your fingers!"

"Don't worry," I tell her. "We'll be perfect swan maidens."

The swan maidens gather in a circle around Lilly. Then we sail across the stage, telling our story.

Our white feathers fan out as we float through the air like flying birds. When we are girls we glide gently across the stage.

I see Pa wink at me in the audience, but I have to be a swan maiden right now, so I can't wink back. Then we slowly move to the back of the stage.

Odette is alone. She is sad and then T.J. — I mean the prince — comes. They dance together, and you can see their joy.

The prince lifts Odette, twirling her around. T.J. looks so handsome and doesn't even mess up, not once.

I can't believe it! T.J. might just be a dancer after all!

Suddenly, they leap gracefully across the stage and duck through the curtain.

Odette and her prince have flown away to escape the evil spell.

Now it's our turn to dance. The swan maidens leap with joy as the curtain goes down.

Then it goes up again, and we all stand on the stage, holding hands, to take a bow. T.J. is holding my hand.

I see Uncle Bay smiling and clapping for me. Momma blows me kisses. Mr. Jim is waving. Daddy is shouting, "Bravo."

T.J. gives my hand a little squeeze.

Then he bends down and whispers in my ear, "You know, Kylie Jean, a swan maiden can grow up to be a queen."

I want to give him a big ole hug, but he wouldn't like it in front of all of these people. I'll save that hug for Ugly Brother later.

I blow kisses to all my fans in the front row. They deserve some sugar for coming to our ballet. Then, just as the curtain starts to go down, I can't resist. I give a little beauty queen wave, nice and slow, side to side.

I'm pretty sure that T.J. is right. I am going to grow up to be a queen.

Marci Bales Peschke was born in Indiana, grew up in Florida, and now lives in Texas with her husband, two children, and a feisty black-and-white cat named Phoebe. She loves reading and watching movies.

When **Tuesday Mourning** was a little girl, she knew she wanted to be an artist when she grew up. Now, she is an illustrator who lives in South Pasadena, CA. She especially loves illustrating books for kids and teenagers. When she isn't illustrating, Tuesday loves spending time with her husband, who is an actor, and their two sons.

Glossary

audition (aw-DISH-uhn)—a short performance by an actor, singer, musician, or dancer to see if he or she is the right person for a role

barre (BAR)—a bar at waist level that dancers use for support while practicing

dress rehearsal (DRES ri-HURS-uhl)—the last rehearsal, in full costume

natural (NACH-ur-uhl)—a person who is good at something because of a special talent or ability

pirouette (pir-oh-ET)—a spin on one foot, with the raised foot touching the other knee

plié (plee-AY)—a movement in which a dancer bends his or her knees and then straightens them again, usually with the heels turned out and the feet on the ground

prima ballerina (PREE-muh bal-uh-REE-nuh)—the main dancer

recital (ri-SYE-tuhl)—a performance

trance (TRANSS)—if you are in a trance, you are not aware of what is going on around you

1. Kylie Jean didn't get the part she wanted. Do you think she ended up being happy or sad about it? Talk about your answer.

2. Kylie Jean and her brother work together to solve the ballet's problems. What do you do with your siblings?

3. What do you think happens after this story ends? Talk about it!

Be Creative!

1. Kylie Jean's goal is to be a beauty queen. What's your number-one dream?

2. Who is your favorite character in this story? Draw a picture of that person. Then write a list of five things you know about them.

3. Design your own ballerina's costume. What color would your tutu be?

This cake is just perfect for any dancing queen!
Just make sure to ask a grown-up for help.

Love, Kylie Jean

From Momma's Kitchen

BALLERINA SLIPPER CAKE

YOU NEED:

1 box of your favorite cake mix (plus eggs and oil as instructed)

1 can of white frosting

Red food coloring

1 piece of waxed paper

1 pencil

1 sharp cake knife

A grown-up helper

Red licorice strings

1. With your grown-up helper, bake your cake, following the instructions for a 13x9 pan. Cool.

2. Use the pencil and waxed paper to trace the shape of two ballerina slippers—one left, one right. Cut out shapes. When cake is completely cool, ask your grown-up helper to use the shapes to cut out two slippers from the cake.

3. Use half of frosting to decorate the middle part of each slipper. Mix remaining half of frosting with a few drops of red food coloring. Spread over remainder of cake. Tie two licorice strings into bows and decorate toes. Yum yum!

Kylie Jean

has one BIG dream . . .
to be a beauty queen!

Available from Picture Window Books
www.capstonepub.com

THE FUN DOESN'T STOP HERE!

Discover more at www.capstonekids.com

♥ Videos & Contests

❀ Games & Puzzles

♥ Friends & Favorites

❀ Authors & Illustrators

Find cool websites and more books like this one at www.facthound.com. Just type in the Book ID: **9781404867987** and you're ready to go!